Marx Machiavelli Chesterton Emerson Joyce
Abbott Hardy Montaigne Cooper Austen
Defoe Melville Haggard Hugo
Christie Eliot Grimm
Stoker Carroll Molière
Wilde Maupassant Byron
Schiller
Garnett Einstein Fitzgerald Engels
Goethe Hawthorne Smith Kafka
Cotton Dostoyevsky Hall
Baum Kipling Doyle Willis
Leslie Dumas Henry Nietzsche
Flaubert Turgenev Balzac
Stockton Vatsyayana Crane
Burroughs Whitman Verne
Curtis Tocqueville Gogol Vinci
Homer Widger Tolstoy Busch
Darwin Thoreau Scott
Potter Freud Zola Twain Plato
Lawrence
Kant Jowett Stevenson Dickens
Andersen Cervantes Burton Hesse Harte
London Descartes
Poe Aristotle Wells Voltaire
Hale James Hastings Cooke
Bunner Shakespeare
Richter Chambers Irving
Doré Swift Dante Chekhov da Shaw Wodehouse Benedict Alcott
Pushkin
Newton

The Red Flower Poems Written in War Time

Henry Van Dyke

Imprint

This book is part of TREDITION CLASSICS

Author: Henry Van Dyke
Cover design: Buchgut, Berlin – Germany

Publisher: tredition GmbH, Hamburg - Germany
ISBN: 978-3-8424-6740-8

www.tredition.com
www.tredition.de

The intention of the TREDITION CLASSICS series is to make world literature in the public domain available in printed format. Literary enthusiasts and organizations, such as Project Gutenberg, worldwide have scanned and digitally edited the original texts. tredition has subsequently formatted and redesigned the content into a modern reading layout. Therefore, we cannot guarantee the exact reproduction of the original format of a particular historic edition. Please also note that no modifications have been made to the spelling, therefore it may differ from the orthography used today.

Produced by Ted Garvin, Tonya Allen and PG Distributed Proofreaders

THE RED FLOWER

POEMS WRITTEN IN WAR TIME

BY HENRY VAN DYKE D.O.L. (OXON.)

1919

PREFACE

These are verses that came to me in this dreadful war time amid the cares and labors of a heavy task.

Two of the poems, "A Scrap of Paper" and "Stand Fast," were written in 1914 and bore the signature *Civis Americanus*—the use of my own name at the time being impossible. Two others, "Lights Out" and "Remarks about Kings," were read for me by Robert Underwood Johnson at the meeting of the American Academy in Boston, November, 1915, at which I was unable to be present.

The rest of the verses were printed after I had resigned my diplomatic post and was free to say what I thought and felt, without reserve.

The "Interludes in Holland" are thoughts of the peaceful things that will abide for all the world after we have won this war against war.

SYLVANORA, October 1, 1917.

CONTENTS

PREMONITION

THE RED FLOWER

June 1914

In the pleasant time of Pentecost,
By the little river Kyll,
I followed the angler's winding path
Or waded the stream at will.
And the friendly fertile German land
Lay round me green and still.

But all day long on the eastern bank
Of the river cool and clear,
Where the curving track of the double rails
Was hardly seen though near,
The endless trains of German troops
Went rolling down to Trier.

They packed the windows with bullet heads
And caps of hodden gray;
They laughed and sang and shouted loud
When the trains were brought to a stay;
They waved their hands and sang again
As they went on their iron way.

No shadow fell on the smiling land,
No cloud arose in the sky;

I could hear the river's quiet tune
  When the trains had rattled by;
But my heart sank low with a heavy sense
  Of trouble,—I knew not why.

Then came I into a certain field
  Where the devil's paint-brush spread
'Mid the gray and green of the rolling hills
  A flaring splotch of red,
An evil omen, a bloody sign,
  And a token of many dead.

I saw in a vision the field-gray horde
  Break forth at the devil's hour,
And trample the earth into crimson mud
  In the rage of the Will to Power,—
All this I dreamed in the valley of Kyll,
  At the sign of the blood-red flower.

A SCRAP OF PAPER

"Will you go to war just for a scrap of paper?" —*Question of the German Chancellor to the British Ambassador, August 3, 1914.*

A mocking question! Britain's answer came
Swift as the light and searching as the flame.

"Yes, for a scrap of paper we will fight
Till our last breath, and God defend the right!

"A scrap of paper where a name is set
Is strong as duty's pledge and honor's debt.

"A scrap of paper holds for man and wife
The sacrament of love, the bound of life.

"A scrap of paper may be Holy Writ
With God's eternal word to hallow it.

"A scrap of paper binds us both to stand
Defenders of a neutral neighbor land.

"By God, by faith, by honor, yes! We fight
To keep our name upon that paper white."

September, 1914

STAND FAST

Stand fast, Great Britain!
Together England, Scotland, Ireland stand
One in the faith that makes a mighty land,
True to the bond you gave and will not break
And fearless in the fight for conscience' sake!
Against Giant Robber clad in steel,
With blood of trampled Belgium on his heel,
Striding through France to strike you down at last,
Britain, stand fast!

Stand fast, brave land!
The Huns are thundering toward the citadel;
They prate of Culture but their path is Hell;
Their light is darkness, and the bloody sword
They wield and worship is their only Lord.
O land where reason stands secure on right,
O land where freedom is the source of light,
Against the mailed Barbarians' deadly blast,
Britain, stand fast!

Stand fast, dear land!
Thou island mother of a world-wide race,
Whose children speak thy tongue and love thy face,
Their hearts and hopes are with thee in the strife,
Their hands will break the sword that seeks thy life;
Fight on until the Teuton madness cease;
Fight bravely on, until the word of peace
Is spoken in the English tongue at last,
Britain, stand fast!

September, 1914.

LIGHTS OUT

(1915)

"Lights out" along the land,
"Lights out" upon the sea.
The night must put her hiding hand
O'er peaceful towns where children sleep,
And peaceful ships that darkly creep
Across the waves, as if they were not free.

The dragons of the air,
The hell-hounds of the deep,
Lurking and prowling everywhere,
Go forth to seek their helpless prey,
Not knowing whom they maim or slay –
Mad harvesters, who care not what they reap.

Out with the tranquil lights,
Out with the lights that burn
For love and law and human rights!
Set back the clock a thousand years:
All they have gained now disappears,
And the dark ages suddenly return.

Kaiser who loosed wild death
And terror in the night
God grant you draw no quiet breath,
Until the madness you began
Is ended, and long-suffering man,
Set free from war lords, cries, "Let there be Light."

October, 1915.

Read at the meeting of the American Academy, Boston, November, 1915.

REMARKS ABOUT KINGS

God said, "I am tired of kings."—EMERSON.

God said, "I am tired of kings,"—
But that was a long time ago!
And meantime man said, "No,
I like their looks in their robes and rings."
So he crowned a few more,
And they went on playing the game as before
Fighting and spoiling things.

Man said, "I am tired of kings!
Sons of the robber-chiefs of yore,
They make me pay for their lust and their war;
I am the puppet, they pull the strings;
The blood of my heart is the wine they drink.
I will govern myself for while I think,
And see what that brings!"

Then God, who made the first remark,
Smiled in the dark.

Read at the meeting of the American Academy, Boston.
November, 1915.

WAR-MUSIC

Break off! Dance no more!
Danger is at the door.
Music is in arms.
To signal war's alarms,

Hark, a sudden trumpet calling
Over the hill
Why are you calling, trumpet, calling?
What is your will?

Men, men, men!
Men who are ready to fight
For their country's life, and the right.
Of a liberty-loving land to be
Free, free, free!
Free from a tyrant's chain,
Free from dishonor's stain,
Free to guard and maintain
All that her fathers fought for,
All that her sons have wrought for,
Resolute, brave, and free!

Call again, trumpet, call again,
Call up the men!
Do you hear the storm of cheers
Mingled with the women's tears
And the tramp, tramp, tramp of marching feet?
Do you hear the throbbing drum
As the hosts of battle come
Keeping time, time, time to its beat?
O Music give a song

To make their spirit strong
For the fury of the tempest they must meet.

The hoarse roar
Of the monster guns;
And the sharp bark
Of the lesser guns;
The whine of the shells,
The rifles' clatter
Where the bullets patter,
The rattle, rattle, rattle
Of the mitrailleuse in battle,
And the yells
Of the men who charge through hells
Where the poison gas descends.
And the bursting shrapnel rends
Limb from limb
In the dim
Chaos and clamor of the strife
Where no man thinks of his life
But only of fighting through,
Blindly fighting through, through!

'Tis done
At last!
The victory won,
The dissonance of warfare past!

O Music mourn the dead
Whose loyal blood was shed,
And sound the taps for every hero slain;
Then lend into the song
That made their spirit strong,
And tell the world they did not die in vain.

Thank God we can see, in the glory of morn,
The invincible flag that our fathers defended;

And our hearts can repeat what the heroes have sworn,
  That war shall not end till the war-lust is ended,
Then the bloodthirsty sword shall no longer be lord
  Of the nations oppressed by the conqueror's horde,
But the banners of freedom shall peacefully wave
  O'er the world of the free and the lands of the brave.

May, 1916

MIGHT AND RIGHT

If Might made Right, life were a wild-beasts' cage;
If Right made Might, this were the golden age;
But now, until we win the long campaign
Right must gain Might to conquer and to reign.

July 1, 1915.

THE PRICE OF PEACE

Peace without Justice is a low estate, –
A coward cringing to an iron Fate!
But Peace through Justice is the great ideal, –
We'll pay the price of war to make it real.

December 28, 1916.

STORM MUSIC

O Music hast thou only heard
The laughing river, the singing bird,
The murmuring wind in the poplar-trees, –
Nothing but Nature's melodies?
  Nay, thou hearest all her tones,
    As a Queen must hear!
    Sounds of wrath and fear,
    Mutterings, shouts, and moans,
  Mildness, tumult, and despair, –
  All she has that shakes the air
  With voices fierce and wild!
Thou art a Queen and not a dreaming child, –
Put on thy crown and let us hear thee reign
Triumphant in a world of storm and strain!

  Echo the long-drawn sighs
Of the mounting wind in the pines,
And the sobs of the mounting waves that rise
  In the dark of the troubled deep
To break on the beach in fiery lines.
  Echo the far-off roll of thunder,
      Rumbling loud
  And ever louder, under
  The blue-black curtain of cloud,
  Where the lightning serpents gleam,
    Echo the moaning
  Of the forest in its sleep
  Like a giant groaning
In the torment of a dream.

  Now an interval of quiet
  For a moment holds the air

In the breathless hush
Of a silent prayer.

Then the sudden rush
Of the rain, and the riot
Of the shrieking, tearing gale
Breaks loose in the night,
With a fusillade of hail!
Hear the forest fight,
With its tossing arms that crack and clash
In the thunder's cannonade,
While the lightning's forkèd flash
Brings the old hero-trees to the ground with a crash!
Hear the breakers' deepening roar,
Driven like a herd of cattle
In the wild stampede of battle,
Trampling, trampling, trampling, to overwhelm the shore.

Is it the end of all?
Will the land crumble and fall?
Nay, for a voice replies
Out of the hidden skies,
"Thus far, O sea, shalt thou go,
So long, O wind, shalt thou blow:
Return to your bounds and cease,
And let the earth have peace!"

O Music, lead the way—
The stormy night is past,
Lift up our heads to greet the day,
And the joy of things that last.

The dissonance and pain
That mortals must endure
Are changed in thine immortal strain
To something great and pure.

True love will conquer strife,
And strength from conflict flows,
For discord is the thorn of life
And harmony the rose.

May, 1916.

FRANCE AND BELGIUM

THE BELLS OF MALINES

AUGUST 17, 1914

The gabled roofs of old Malines
Are russet red and gray and green,
And o'er them in the sunset hour
Looms, dark and huge, St. Rombold's tower.
High in that rugged nest concealed,
The sweetest bells that ever pealed,
The deepest bells that ever rung,
The lightest bells that ever sung,
Are waiting for the master's hand
To fling their music o'er the land.

And shall they ring to-night, Malines?
In nineteen hundred and fourteen,
The frightful year, the year of woe,
When fire and blood and rapine flow
Across the land from lost Liége,
Storm-driven by the German rage?
The other carillons have ceased;
Fallen is Hasselt, fallen Diesl,
From Ghent and Bruges no voices come,
Antwerp is silent, Brussels dumb!

But in thy belfry, O Malines,
The master of the bells unseen
Has climbed to where the keyboard stands,—
To-night his heart is in his hands!
Once more, before invasion's hell
Breaks round the tower he loves so well,
Once more he strikes the well-worn keys,
And sends aërial harmonies
Far-floating through the twilight dim
In patriot song and holy hymn.

O listen, burghers of Malines!
Soldier and workman, pale béguine.
And mother with a trembling flock
Of children clinging to thy frock,—
Look up and listen, listen all!
What tunes are these that gently fall
Around you like a benison?
"The Flemish Lion," "Brabançonne,"
"O brave Liége," and all the airs
That Belgium in her bosom bears.

Ring up, ye silvery octaves high,
Whose notes like circling swallows fly;
And ring, each old sonorous bell,—
"Jesu," "Maria," "Michaël!"
Weave in and out, and high and low,
The magic music that you know,
And let it float and flutter down
To cheer the heart of the troubled town.
Ring out, "Salvator," lord of all,—
"Roland" in Ghent may hear thee call!

O brave bell-music of Malines,
In this dark hour how much you mean!
The dreadful night of blood and tears
Sweeps down on Belgium, but she hears

Deep in her heart the melody
Of songs she learned when she was free.
She will not falter, faint, nor fail,
But fight until her rights prevail
And all her ancient belfries ring
"The Flemish Lion," "God Save the King!"

THE NAME OF FRANCE

Give us a name to fill the mind
With the shining thoughts that lead mankind,
The glory of learning, the joy of art,—
A name that tells of a splendid part.
In long, long toil and the strenuous fight
Of the human race to win its way
From the feudal darkness into the day
Of Freedom, Brotherhood, Equal Right,—
A name like a star, a name of light.
I give you *France*!

Give us a name to stir the blood
With a warmer glow and a swifter flood,
At the touch of a courage that knows not fear,—
A name like the sound of a trumpet, clear.
And silver-sweet, and iron-strong,
That calls three million men to their feet,
Ready to march, and steady to meet
The foes who threaten that name with wrong,—
A name that rings like a battle-song.
I give you *France*!

Give us a name to move the heart
With the strength that noble griefs impart,
A name that speaks of the blood outpoured
To save mankind from the sway of the sword,—
A name that calls on the world to share
In the burden of sacrificial strife
When the cause at stake is the world's free life
And the rule of the people everywhere,—
A name like a vow, a name like a prayer.

I give you *France*!

The Hague, September, 1916.

JEANNE D'ARC RETURNS

1914 1916

What hast thou done, O womanhood of France,
  Mother and daughter, sister, sweetheart, wife,
  What hast thou done, amid this fateful strife,
To prove the pride of thine inheritance.
In this fair land of freedom and romance?
  I hear thy voice with tears and courage rife, –
  Smiling against the swords that seek thy life –
Make answer in a noble utterance:
"I give France all I have, and all she asks.
  Would it were more! Ah, let her ask and take;
My hands to nurse her wounded, do her tasks, –
  My feet to run her errands through the dark, –
My heart to bleed in triumph for her sake, –
  And all my soul to follow thee, Jeanne d'Arc!"

April 16, 1916.

INTERLUDES IN HOLLAND

THE HEAVENLY HILLS OF HOLLAND

The heavenly hills of Holland,—
  How wondrously they rise
Above the smooth green pastures
  Into the azure skies!
With blue and purple hollows,
  With peaks of dazzling snow,
Along the far horizon
  The clouds are marching slow,

No mortal fool has trodden
  The summits of that range,
Nor walked those mystic valleys
  Whose colors ever change;
Yet we possess their beauty,
  And visit them in dreams,
While the ruddy gold of sunset
  From cliff and canyon gleams.

In days of cloudless weather
  They melt into the light;
When fog and mist surround us
  They're hidden from our sight;
But when returns a season
  Clear shining after rain,
While the northwest wind is blowing,

We see the hills again.

The old Dutch painters loved them,
Their pictures show them clear,—
Old Hobbema and Ruysduel,
Van Goyen and Vermeer,
Above the level landscape,
Rich polders, long-armed mills,
Canals and ancient cities,—
Float Holland's heavenly hills.

The Hague, November, 1916.

THE PROUD LADY

When Stävoren town was in its prime
 And queened the Zuyder Zee,
Its ships went out to every clime
 With costly merchantry.

A lady dwelt in that rich town,
 The fairest in all the land;
She walked abroad in a velvet gown,
 With many rings on her hand.

Her hair was bright as the beaten gold,
 Her lips as coral red,
Her roving eyes were blue and bold,
 And her heart with pride was fed.

For she was proud of her father's ships,
 As she watched them gayly pass;
And pride looked out of her eyes and lips
 When she saw herself in the glass.

"Now come," she said to the captains ten,
 Who were ready to put to sea,
"Ye are all my men and my father's men,
 And what will ye do for me?"

"Go north and south, go east and west,
 And get me gifts," she said.
"And he who bringeth me home the best,
 With that man will I wed."

So they all fared forth, and sought with care
In many a famous mart,
For satins and silks and jewels rare,
To win that lady's heart.

She looked at them all with never a thought
And careless put them by;
"I am not fain of the things ye brought,
Enough of these have I."

The last that came was the head of the fleet,
His name was Jan Borel;
He bent his knee at the lady's feet,—
In truth he loved her well.

"I've brought thee home the best i' the world,
A shipful of Danzig corn!"
She stared at him long; her red lips curled,
Her blue eyes filled with scorn.

"Now out on thee, thou feckless kerl,
A loon thou art," she said.
"Am I a starving beggar girl?
Shall I ever lack for bread?"

"Go empty all thy sacks of grain
Into the nearest sea,
And never show thy face again
To make a mock of me."

Young Jan Borel, he answered naught,
But in the harbor cast
The sacks of golden corn he brought,
And groaned when fell the last.

Then Jan Borel, he hoisted sail,
 And out to sea he bore;
He passed the Helder in a gale
 And came again no more.

But the grains of corn went drifting down
 Like devil-scattered seed,
To sow the harbor of the town
 With a wicked growth of weed.

The roots were thick and the silt and sand
 Were gathered day by day,
Till not a furlong out from land
 A shoal had barred the way.

Then Stävoren town saw evil years,
 No ships could out or in.
The boats lay rolling at the piers,
 And the mouldy grain in the bin.

The grass-grown streets were all forlorn,
 The town in ruin stood,
The lady's velvet gown was torn,
 Her rings were sold for food.

Her father had perished long ago,
 But the lady held her pride.
She walked with a scornful step and slow,
 Till at last in her rags she died.

Yet still on the crumbling piers of the town,
 When the midnight moon shines free,
A woman walks in a velvet gown
 And scatters corn in the sea.

FLOOD-TIDE OF FLOWERS

IN HOLLAND

The laggard winter ebbed so slow
With freezing rain and melting snow,
It seemed as if the earth would stay
Forever where the tide was low,
In sodden green and watery gray.

But now from depths beyond our sight,
The tide is turning in the night,
And floods of color long concealed
Come silent rising toward the light,
Through garden bare and empty field.

And first, along the sheltered nooks,
The crocus runs in little brooks
Of joyance, till by light made bold
They show the gladness of their looks
In shining pools of white and gold.

The tiny scilla, sapphire blue,
Is gently sweeping in, to strew
The earth with heaven; and sudden rills
Of sunlit yellow, sweeping through,
Spread into lakes of daffodils.

The hyacinths, with fragrant heads,
Have overflowed their sandy beds,
And fill the earth with faint perfume,
The breath that Spring around her sheds.

And now the tulips break in bloom!

A sea, a rainbow-tinted sea,
A splendor and a mystery,
Floods o'er the fields of faded gray:
The roads are full of folks in glee,
For lo,—to-day is Easter Day!

April, 1916.

ENTER AMERICA

AMERICA'S PROSPERITY

They tell me thou art rich, my country: gold
 In glittering flood has poured into thy chest;
 Thy flocks and herds increase, thy barns are pressed
With harvest, and thy stores can hardly hold
Their merchandise; unending trains are rolled
 Along thy network rails of East and West;
 Thy factories and forges never rest;
Thou art enriched in all things bought and sold!

But dost *thou* prosper? Better news I crave.
 O dearest country, is it well with thee
  Indeed, and is thy soul in health?
A nobler people, hearts more wisely brave,
 And thoughts that lift men up and make them free.—
  These are prosperity and vital wealth!

The Hague, October 1, 1916.

THE GLORY OF SHIPS

The glory of ships is an old, old song,
 since the days when the sea-rovers ran
In their open boats through the roaring surf,
 and the spread of the world began;
The glory of ships is a light on the sea,
 and a star in the story of man.

When Homer sang of the galleys of Greece
 that conquered the Trojan shore,
And Solomon lauded the barks of Tyre that
 brought great wealth to his door,
'Twas little they knew, those ancient men,
 what would come of the sail and the oar.

The Greek ships rescued the West from the East,
 when they harried the Persians home;
And the Roman ships were the wings of strength
 that bore up the empire, Rome;
And the ships or Spain found a wide new world
 far over the fields of foam.

Then the tribes of courage at last saw clear
 that the ocean was not a bound,
But a broad highway, and a challenge to seek
 for treasure as yet unfound;
So the fearless ships fared forth to the search,
 in joy that the globe was round.

Their hulls were heightened, their sails spread out.
 they grew with the growth of their quest;
They opened the secret doors of the East,

and the golden gates of the West;
And many a city of high renown
was proud of a ship on its crest.

The fleets of England and Holland and France
were at strife with each other and Spain;
And battle and storm sent a myriad ships
to sleep in the depths of the main;
But the seafaring spirit could never be drowned,
and it filled up the fleets again.

They greatened and grew, with the aid of steam,
to a wonderful, vast array,
That carries the thoughts and the traffic of men
into every harbor and bay;
And now in the world-wide work of the ships
'tis England that leads the way.

O well for the leading that follows the law
of a common right on the sea!
But ill for the leader who tries to hold
what belongs to mankind in fee!
The way of the ships is an open way,
and the ocean must ever be free!

Remember, O first of the maritime folk,
how the rise of your greatness began.
It will live if you safeguard the round-the-world road
from the shame of a selfish ban;
For the glory of ships is a light on the sea,
and a star in the story of man!

September 12, 1916.

MARE LIBERUM

I

You dare to say with perjured lips,
"We fight to make the ocean free"?
You, whose black trail of butchered ships
Bestrews the bed of every sea
Where German submarines have wrought
Their horrors! Have you never thought,—
What you call freedom, men call piracy!

II

Unnumbered ghosts that haunt the wave,
Where you have murdered, cry you down;
And seamen whom you would not save,
Weave now in weed grown depths a crown
Of shame for your imperious head,—
A dark memorial of the dead,—
Women and children whom you sent to drown.

III

Nay, not till thieves are set to guard
The gold, and corsairs called to keep
O'er peaceful commerce watch and ward
And wolves do herd the helpless sheep,
Shall men and women look to thee,
Thou ruthless Old Man of the Sea,
To safeguard law and freedom on the deep!

IV

In nobler breeds we put our trust;
The nations in whose sacred lore
The "Ought" stands out above the "Must,"
And honor rules in peace and war.
With these we hold in soul and heart,
With these we choose our lot and part,
Till Liberty is safe on sea and shore.

London Times, February 12, 1917.

"LIBERTY ENLIGHTENING THE WORLD"

Thou warden of the western gate, above Manhattan Bay,
The fogs of doubt that hid thy face are driven clean away:
Thine eyes at last look far and clear, thou liftest high thy hand
To spread the light of liberty world-wide for every land.

No more thou dreamest of a peace reserved alone for thee,
While friends are fighting for thy cause beyond the guardian sea;
The battle that they wage is thine; thou fallest if they fall;
The swollen flood of Prussian pride will sweep unchecked o'er all.

O cruel is the conquer-lust in Hohenzollern brains;
The paths they plot to gain their goal are dark with shameful stains:
No faith they keep, no law revere, no god but naked Might;—
They are the foemen of mankind. Up, Liberty; and smite!

Britain, and France, and Italy, and Russia newly born,
Have waited for thee in the night. Oh, come as comes the morn!
Serene and strong and full of faith, America, arise,
With steady hope and mighty help to join thy brave Allies.

O dearest country of my heart, home of the high desire,
Make clean thy soul for sacrifice on Freedom's altar-fire;
For thou must suffer, thou must fight, until the war-lords cease,
And all the peoples lift their heads in liberty and peace.

London Times, April 12, 1917.

THE OXFORD THRUSHES

FEBRUARY, 1917

I never thought again to hear
The Oxford thrushes singing clear,
Amid the February rain,
Their sweet, indomitable strain.

A wintry vapor lightly spreads
Among the trees, and round the beds
Where daffodil and jonquil sleep,
Only the snowdrop wakes to weep.

It is not springtime yet. Alas,
What dark, tempestuous days must pass,
Till England's trial by battle cease,
And summer comes again with peace.

The lofty halls, the tranquil towers,
Where Learning in untroubled hours
Held her high court, serene in fame,
Are lovely still, yet not the same.

The novices in fluttering gown
No longer fill the ancient town,
But fighting men in khaki drest—
And in the Schools the wounded rest.

Ah, far away, 'neath stranger skies
Full many a son of Oxford lies,
And whispers from his warrior grave,

"I died to keep the faith you gave."

The mother mourns, but does not fail,
Her courage and her love prevail
O'er sorrow, and her spirit hears
The promise of triumphant years.

Then sing, ye thrushes, in the rain
Your sweet, indomitable strain.
Ye bring a word from God on high
And voices in our hearts reply.

HOMEWARD BOUND

Home, for my heart still calls me;
 Home, through the danger zone;
Home, whatever befalls me,
 I will sail again to my own!

Wolves of the sea are hiding
 Closely along the way,
Under the water biding
 Their moment to rend and slay.

Black is the eagle that brands them,
 Black are their hearts as the night,
Black is the hate that sends them
 To murder but not to fight.

Flower of the German Culture,
 Boast of the Kaiser's Marine,
Choose for your emblem the vulture,
 Cowardly, cruel, obscene!

Forth from her sheltered haven
 Our peaceful ship glides slow,
Noiseless in flight as a raven,
 Gray as a hoodie crow.

She doubles and turns in her bearing,
 Like a twisting plover she goes;
The way of her westward faring
 Only the captain knows.

In a lonely bay concealing
  She lingers for days, and slips
At dusk from her covert, stealing
  Thro' channels feared by the ships.

Brave are the men, and steady,
  Who guide her over the deep,—
British mariners, ready
  To face the sea-wolf's leap.

Lord of the winds and waters,
  Bring our ship to her mark,
Safe from this game of hide-and-seek
  With murderers in the dark!

On the S.S. *Baltic*, May, 1917.